key to reading

At Key Porter Kids, we understand how important reading is to a young child's development. That's why we created the Key to Reading program, a structured approach to reading for the beginner. While the books in this series are educational, they are also engaging and fun – key elements in gaining and retaining a child's interest. Plus, with each level in the program designed for different reading abilities, children can advance at their own pace and become successful, confident readers in the process.

Level 1: The Beginner

For children familiar with the alphabet and ready to begin reading.
- Very large type
- Simple words
- Short sentences
- Repetition of key words
- Picture cues
- Colour associations
- Directional reading
- Picture match-up cards

Level 2: The Emerging Reader

For children able to recognize familiar words on sight and sound out new words with help.
- Large type
- Easy words
- Longer sentences
- Repetition of key words and phrases
- Picture cues
- Context cues
- Directional reading
- Picture and word match-up cards

Level 3: The Independent Reader

For increasingly confident readers who can sound out new words on their own.
- Large type
- Expanded vocabulary
- Longer sentences and paragraphs
- Repetition of longer words and phrases
- Picture cues
- Context cues
- More complex storylines
- Flash cards

Max was playing cowboy.

Ruby was trying to write a story.
"Once upon a time, there was a..."

"Cowboy!" yelled Max.
Max played a song on his
silver harmonica.

"I'm sorry, Max," said Ruby.
"I can't play cowboy now.
I'm trying to write a story."

Max played cowboy
with his yellow chicks.

Ruby started her story again.
"Once upon a time, there was a..."

"Cowboy!" yelled Max.
Max herded the yellow chicks
through the kitchen.

"I'm sorry, Max," said Ruby.
"I can't play cowboy now.
I'm trying to write a story."

Max played cowboy
with his red lobster.

Ruby started her story again.
"Once upon a time, there was a..."

"Cowboy!" yelled Max.
Max lassoed his red lobster.

"I'm sorry, Max," said Ruby.
"I'm trying to write a story,
but you keep interrupting."

"First, you played your harmonica.
Next, you herded your yellow chicks
through the kitchen."

"Then, you lassoed your red lobster.
No wonder I can't think of what
comes next in my story."

"I only get to start my story:
Once upon a time, there was a..."

"Cowboy!" yelled Max.

"That's it, Max!" said Ruby.
"I know what to write.
And you can help me."

Ruby started her story again:
"Once upon a time, there was a..."

"Cowboy!" yelled Max,
finishing the first line of Ruby's story.

Max

Max

Lobster

Lobster

Chicks

Chicks

Ruby

Ruby

CUT ALONG DOTTED LINES

Hat

Hat

Horse

Horse